SO-BNV-530

"I DON'T LIKE CHOOSE YOUR OWN ADVENTURE® BOOKS. I *LOVE* THEM!" says Jessica Gordon, age ten. And now kids between the ages of six and nine can choose their own adventures too. Here's what kids have to say about the Skylark Choose Your Own Adventure® books.

"These are my favorite books because you can pick whatever choice you want— and the story is all about you."
—**Katy Alson,** *age 8*

"I love finding out how my story will end."
—**Joss Williams,** *age 9*

"I like all the illustrations!"
—**Savitri Brightfield,** *age 7*

"A six-year-old friend and I have lots of fun making the decisions together."
—**Peggy Marcus** *(adult)*

Bantam Books in the Skylark Choose Your Own
   Adventure® Series
Ask your bookseller for the books you have missed

HAUNTED HALLOWEEN PARTY

SUSAN SAUNDERS

ILLUSTRATED BY RON WING

An Edward Packard Book

A BANTAM SKYLARK BOOK®
NEW YORK · TORONTO · LONDON · SYDNEY · AUCKLAND

RL 2, 007–009

HAUNTED HALLOWEEN PARTY

A Bantam Skylark Book / October 1986

4 printings through August 1989

*CHOOSE YOUR OWN ADVENTURE® is a registered trademark of
Bantam Books.*

*Skylark Books is a registered trademark of Bantam Books,
a division of Bantam Doubleday Dell Publishing Group, Inc.
Registered in U.S. Patent and Trademark Office and elsewhere.*

ISBN 0-553-15453-2

Published simultaneously in the United States and Canada

*Bantam Books are published by Bantam Books, a division of Ban-
tam Doubleday Dell Publishing Group. Inc. Its trademark, consisting
of the words "Bantam Books" and the portrayal of a rooster, is
Registered in U.S. Patent and Trademark Office and in other coun-
tries. Marca Registrada. Bantam Books, 666 Fifth Avenue, New
York, New York 10103.*

PRINTED IN THE UNITED STATES OF AMERICA

CW   13   12   11   10   9   8   7   6   5   4

For Justin Brooks

READ THIS FIRST!!!

Most books are about other people.

This book is about you—and a strange Halloween party.

What happens to you at the party depends on what you decide to do.

Do not read this book from the first page through to the last page. Instead, start on page one and read until you come to your first choice. Then turn to the page shown and see what happens.

When you come to the end of a story, go back and start again. Every choice leads to a new adventure.

Are you ready to go to the Halloween party? Then turn to page one—and good luck!

It's Halloween night. You and your older sister, Nancy, have been invited to a costume party. Some friends are holding it at the Brill mansion—a creepy, old house that no one has lived in for years.

You are going as a creature from outer space. Your mask is blue and scaly. It has a snout, three eyes, and floppy ears.

Nancy is dressed as a witch. She is wearing a black robe and a pointed black hat. Her mask has a long, skinny nose with a bump on the end of it.

Your father drives you and Nancy to the party. He stops the car outside an iron gate. "Just walk up the brick path," he says. "The mansion is at the top of the hill."

You and Nancy climb out of the car.

"I'll pick you up here after the party," your father says. "Have a good time!"

You head up the hill. Leaves rustle in the wind. Clouds slide past the moon. It's spooky here.

"Look," Nancy says, squeezing through some bushes. "I'll bet this is a shortcut."

Turn to page 2.

2   You push your way through, too. You don't see Nancy on the other side. But you find a path that leads to an old house.

Inside, the party has started. You bump into a short ghost in a sheet. "Sorry," you say.

But the sheet drops to the floor. And . . . oh, my gosh! There's no one under it!

You look at the skeletons, trolls, and goblins. They're not . . . wearing . . . costumes—they're real!

This can't be the Brill mansion! You'd better find Nancy and get out of here! Across the room you see two witches. But which witch is your sister? Is she the witch bobbing for apples? Or the witch stroking a black cat? What if neither witch is Nancy?

If you think the witch bobbing for apples is Nancy, turn to page 18.

If you think Nancy is the witch stroking the cat, turn to page 12.

If you think neither witch is Nancy, turn to page 26.

4   You've hardly taken three steps when a voice mutters, "Hey! Where are we going?"

Who is talking? You don't see anyone, but someone must have seen you. You'd better pretend you're just looking around. "I thought I'd check out the cellar," you say calmly.

"But I want to go back to the party!" the voice whines. Who is it?

Suddenly, you feel something pressing down on your hand. The jack-o'-lantern's teeth are closing on your fingers!

"Ouch!" you yelp. You drop the pumpkin.

"Ow!" it groans. It bounces down the stairs yelling, "Help! Someone is trying to squash me!"

That'll bring everybody down here. In fact, here comes a witch! But the witch brushes past you and disappears around a corner.

Her walk reminds you of someone. . . . Nancy! You could follow her. But what if she isn't Nancy?

There's a door in the cellar wall. Could it be another way out of here?

Go on to the next page.

If you follow the witch, turn to page 33.

If you decide to try the door,
turn to page 42.

6   You let go of the witch's arm and back away. But there are dozens of trolls, skeletons, and ghosts between you and the front door. How are you ever going to get out of this house?

Across the room you spot some stairs leading down. There must be a cellar at the bottom of them. Maybe you can find a way out down there. At least you can hide until the party is over.

The cellar stairs look very steep and dark. And it's hard to see well with your mask on. Maybe you should take it off. Then again, maybe it's safer to hide your real face at this weird party.

If you take off your mask, turn to page 25.

If you think it's safer to keep your mask on, turn to page 29.

"No," you say to Nancy. "They'll look in **7** the trunk first thing. Let's climb through the window. Then at least we'll be outside this creepy house."

You push the window open. You crawl out onto the roof. Nancy is right behind you. As soon as she's outside, you hear someone cackle, "Up here! Hurry up! Hurry up!"

Go on to the next page.

In the moonlight, you see more witches—lots of them! They're perched on the peak of the roof. And a short witch is handing out brooms!

Turn to page 15.

"Trick or treat!" the creepy creatures shout. Holding hands, the spooky crew streams out of the house into the moonlight. You have no choice—you have to go with them!

They rush down the hill, past the grocery store. The skeletons shriek, "Wheeee!" And the coffee cans in the grocery store window roll away in fear! Then the ghoulish gang whirls past the library and the barber shop. When the goblins moan, "Eeeee!" a barber pole turns white with fright!

You don't know how long you're dragged around. But suddenly you find yourself in your own neighborhood. Your house is just down the street.

Should you try to lead the creatures to your house? Maybe then you can get yourself out of this mess. Or should you keep this creepy bunch as far away from your house and family as you can?

If you try to lead the creepy crew to your house, turn to page 30.

If you think you should stay away from your house, turn to page 20.

12   Your sister loves cats. She must be the witch stroking the black cat.

Go on to the next page.

You edge around three dancing goblins. **13**
You squeeze past a hairy troll and a glowing
skeleton. Nancy is bending down to pat the
cat, so she doesn't see you. "Nancy!" you
whisper. "Let's go!"

She doesn't answer right away. What if this
witch isn't Nancy after all? But then you hear
your sister's voice from behind her mask:
"This is such a cute cat, isn't it?"

"Forget about the cat!" you groan. "We
have to get out of this house before someone
spots us!"

"What do you mean? We just got here!"
Nancy argues. She hasn't noticed anything
strange going on!

"It's the wrong house! It's the wrong party!"
you whisper. You grab Nancy's arm and start
to pull her toward the front door.

Turn to page 22.

14   You crouch down behind the cellar door. You hope no one else sees you.

But the witch's cries have frightened everybody.

"What scared Abigail?" rattles a skeleton.

"Let's not stick around to find out!" rumbles a short blue goblin.

"We'd better get out of here fast!" shout twin trolls.

Turn to page 41.

"No way I'm going up there," you mutter.

"This is no time to argue!" your sister whispers.

Nancy climbs up the roof, and you follow her.

"Who is this?" the short witch squawks, looking at you.

"Just a friend," Nancy tells her.

"You'd better take this one then," the short witch says. "It has a passenger seat." She hands Nancy a big shovel. "Everyone ready?" she shrieks.

"Ready!" the other witches cry.

"Climb aboard!"

All the witches mount their brooms.

"You'd better do it, too," you whisper to Nancy. "Pretend you're part of the group."

Nancy throws a leg over the handle of the shovel. And you sit down in the scoop part. You'll wait for the witches to fly away. Then the two of you can think about how to get down from the roof.

The witches start chanting something that sounds like "Himl, friml, griml."

Go on to the next page.

They soar off the roof on their brooms! And so do you!

"Now what?" Nancy yells.

There are some large, soft-looking bushes

on the hill just below you. Should you jump
before your shovel flies any higher? Or should
you try to ride the shovel down?

*If you think you should jump,
turn to page 47.*

*If you try to ride the shovel down,
turn to page 50.*

18   Nancy has to be the witch bobbing for apples—she's always hungry! You cross the room as coolly as you can. You don't want anyone in this creepy crowd to decide you're not as spooky as they are.

Nancy is kneeling next to a big silver tub filled with water. "Do you have to bob for apples right now?" you mutter. You tug at her arm.

"Apples!" she squawks. "What apples?"

You stare down at the water. Those aren't apples floating in the tub—they're lumpy gray toads!

And there are two bumps on the end of this witch's nose, not one! It's not Nancy at all. This is a real witch!

Turn to page 6.

You've got to keep this creepy bunch away from your house! But how?

The spooky gang drags you past the Wilsons' gate. You hope the Wilsons don't look out their front window: This group would give them quite a shock. Then you remember Max, the Wilsons' dog.

"Meow!" you call loudly. "Meow! Meow!"

"Meow!" The skeletons and the trolls join

in. They think it's a great new way to scare **21** people.

"Meow!" whine the goblins.

But you know something they don't. Cats make Max *wild*! So wild that he's not afraid of anything!

Turn to page 48.

22 Suddenly, the black cat gives a low growl. Its shape is changing! As you watch, the cat stretches taller: Its nose gets longer and thinner. And its ears grow together . . . into a shiny, pointed hat!

"A real witch!" Nancy squeaks.

"That's why we have to get out of here!" you snap.

But the cat-witch shrieks, "Stop!"

Go on to the next page.

Two goblins block the front door. So you and Nancy dart up the stairs to the second floor.

"They're coming after us!" you yell.

"Let's go in here," Nancy says. You dash into a room draped with cobwebs. A huge trunk stands on one side of the room. There's a round window in the opposite wall.

"We'll hide in the trunk," Nancy tells you.

Won't they find you there? Maybe you should crawl out the window. But you don't remember seeing any trees next to the house. How will you get down?

*If you decide to hide in the trunk,
turn to page 34.*

*If you decide to crawl out the window,
turn to page 7.*

You'll take off your mask when no one's **25**
looking.

The witch's eyes are on the toads. And everyone else in the room is watching some goblins dance. You creep over to the cellar door. Then you pull down your mask.

"Eeeeek!" The witch is staring straight at your face and screaming loudly. "How disgusting! Eeeeek! How did *you* get in here!" She's used to looking at skeletons, trolls, and other witches. But she's not used to seeing a regular kid at this kind of party!

Your real face scares the witch so much that she fades away. In her place is a furry black spider! It scurries behind a chair.

Turn to page 14.

26   You don't think either witch is your sister. One of the witches looks too plump. The other witch looks too tall and thin.

Nancy must have turned off the path. She's probably at the right party, while you're definitely at the wrong one! The best thing you can do is get out of here as fast as you can!

Quietly, you back toward the door. But when you pull it, the door flies open with a bang. All eyes turn to stare at you.

A huge green troll plods slowly toward you. "Is it time?" he asks in a strange, hollow voice.

"Time?" you ask weakly.

"Time!" other voices shriek. "It's time!"

The troll grabs one of your hands. The bony fingers of a skeleton close on the other. "Time to trick or treat!"

Turn to page 11.

Those cellar stairs are awfully dark. And the cellar may be even darker. But taking off your mask could get you into big trouble here.

Then you see a row of jack-o'-lanterns against the wall. Light gleams from their eyes and mouths—candles must be burning inside them. They give you an idea. You'll use one of the jack-o'-lanterns as a flashlight!

You look carefully around the room to make sure no one is watching you. Then you pick up the jack-o'-lantern that gives off the most light, the one with the largest mouth. It has big square eyes and two rows of snaggly teeth. Holding it tightly around the middle, you walk toward the cellar stairs. The pumpkin lights your way as you creep down the steps.

Turn to page 4.

30   You want to go home. That's all there is to it. So you yell as bravely as you can, "This way!" You tug at the skeleton's bony fingers and the troll's hairy hand.

"This way!" the others shout.

Soon you're standing outside your own house. And so is a crowd of trolls and goblins and skeletons and witches—real ones!

"Trick or treat!" a troll rumbles.

The front light is switched on. Your mother steps out onto the porch.

"They'll scare her so badly that her hair will turn white!" you groan to yourself. "And it'll be my fault!"

You have to do something. But what?

Turn to page 39.

The other witch wasn't Nancy, so maybe this one is. You run after her. As you round the corner, the light from the pumpkin fades. It's too dark for you to see anything at all. But you don't turn back.

You stumble forward in the blackness for what seems like hours. The cellar narrows to a tunnel. On either side of you are cold, damp walls.

Suddenly, the tunnel splits in two. You stop, wondering which fork to take. What is that? You think you hear strange, tinkling music. You hold your breath and listen.

There *is* music, coming from the right fork of the tunnel! Then you look up the left fork. You see a patch of gray against the blackness. Could that be a light at the end of it?

If you take the right fork, toward the music, turn to page 36.

If you take the left fork of the tunnel, turn to page 44.

Nancy pulls up the top of the huge trunk. She climbs into it. You jump in after her. Whoooops! Suddenly, you're whizzing down a smooth, slick slide!

The top of the slide was hidden in the trunk. It dives through the walls of the old house. But where does it end? You have a funny feeling. . . .

"Stop!" you shout at your sister.

"I can't!" she yells back.

Neither can you. There's nothing to hang on to!

Whoooosh! You and Nancy shoot off the slide . . . right into the middle of the same creepy party! Skeletons and ghosts, witches and goblins stare down at you. And you look up at them.

"Trick or treat?" you say shakily.

The End

36 You walk to the right, toward the strange music. But the tunnel ends in a stone wall. And the music is coming from the other side of it.

Tunnels sometimes have secret doors. Maybe you can find a latch somewhere. You run your fingers up and down the wall. But you don't feel anything that might open a door.

You're worn out and upset from wandering around in the dark. You give the wall a good kick. Suddenly, it swings open! You tumble forward through a small door into a room filled with lights and music—and witches and trolls!

"The tunnel must have doubled back," you moan. "I'm right where I started!"

You try to run, but a goblin grabs you: "Gotcha!"

You're tired of this. You stamp on the goblin's toe as hard as you can.

"Hey!" cries the goblin. "What did you do that for? It's me—Tommy!"

It's your friend Tommy Keeler—and the Brill mansion—and the right party at last!

The End

"Eeeee!" the spooky crew shrieks at your mother. "Wheeee!" They whirl around on your lawn in a wild dance.

But your mother isn't afraid. In fact, she pays no attention to them at all.

She has spotted you in your blue mask with three eyes and a snout. "You're supposed to be at the party. Nancy just called. She's been looking for you all evening," your mother scolds. "Just what do you think you're doing, wandering around the streets?" She steps onto the lawn and pulls you away from the skeleton and the troll. Without giving them a second look, she tells you: "Go inside, right now!"

She hurries you up the steps and into the house. The door slams behind you, shutting you in—and closing *them* out!

"Straight to bed!" your mother orders. "And no arguments. We'll talk about this in the morning!"

Who's going to argue? Your bed has never looked so good!

The End

The ghosts slip out through the walls of the house like smoke. Everyone else at the party races for the front door. Trolls push goblins out of the way. Skeletons clatter after them. And a black cat rockets over-head on a broom!

"Whew!" you sigh. "Safe!"

There's just one thing you're sorry about. You've always wanted to win a prize for scariest costume. And you have a feeling you couldn't be beaten at this Halloween party!

The End

42   You hope the door leads out of the cellar. You jerk it open, then close it quickly behind you.

But when you turn around, you're not alone. In front of you is a low table. On the table is a glowing glass ball. And behind the table is an old witch!

"Want your fortune told, dearie?" she croaks.

"Uh, n-no thanks," you say.

"Of course you do," she tells you. "Come closer."

The witch peers into the glass ball. You stare at it, too. It gets cloudy for a second. Then it clears.

You see yourself in it! You're wearing your costume. And then you're not! You're in your real clothes, with your real face! Behind you some strange creatures are pointing and muttering.

Nervously, you touch your mask. "I predict," the old witch is saying, "that you're going to have a very scary Halloween!"

The door crashes open behind you. . . .

The End

44　　You walk slowly toward the patch of gray at the end of the left fork. Suddenly, you hear something. First in front of you, but now all around you, there are rustlings and twitterings and squeaks!

You stumble forward in the darkness. You put out your hand to steady yourself . . . and you touch small, furry *bodies*! Bats! There are bats all around you! They've been asleep, stuck to the roof and sides of the tunnel. But now you've awakened them. They're starting to fly!

Turn to page 52.

"Jump!" you tell your sister.   **47**

You slide off the scoop. You're falling . . .
falling . . . falling. You land safely in a big,
plump evergreen bush. Quickly, you roll out
of the way. You don't want Nancy to fall on
top of you.

But Nancy doesn't fall at all! Where is she?

You look up at the moonlit sky. You see
Nancy zoom away on her shovel, just like a
real witch.

Wait a minute. That *was* Nancy . . . wasn't
it?

The End

48 Max sleeps in the backyard. You're sure he'll sneak around the house.

"Grrragh!" Here he comes!

You scramble up onto the Wilsons' car to **49** get out of the way. Max hurls himself at the nearest troll. He rips the troll's jacket right off his back!

Turn to page 54.

50 "Let's try to land this shovel," you shout.

"How?" Nancy yelps.

"Down!" you tell the shovel. But it flies straight ahead.

"Maybe if we lean forward," Nancy says, "it will tilt down." But that doesn't work either.

Then you remember the witches' chant. "What did they say?" you ask your sister. "The chant that made the shovel go—maybe if we turn the words around, the shovel will *stop!*"

"Griml!" your sister says.

"Friml!" you say.

"Himl!" the two of you shout together.

Will it work? At first nothing happens. Then you hang on as the shovel zooms up and up. It's pointed at the moon!

Go on to the next page.

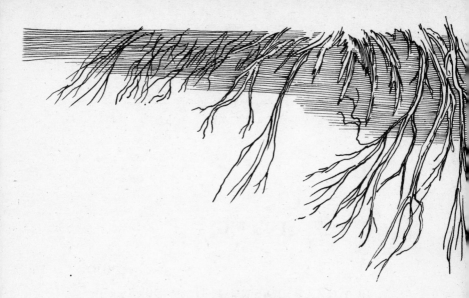

You wonder as you leave the earth far behind: Will you and Nancy and the shovel be-
come just another UFO?
At least you are dressed right . . .

The End

You can feel the bats flapping around you. The tunnel is filled with their squeaking! Ugh! Then you remember: Bats fly out of caves at night to find food. This tunnel must open to the outside!

You cover your head with your arms. You walk quickly up the tunnel toward the patch of gray. Bats are everywhere. Just when you think you can't stand it any longer, you burst out of the tunnel into the moonlight!

On the hill below you, there's a witch. "Nancy?" you call, hurrying toward her. But you stop short, because the witch flaps her arms once, twice. Then, slowly, she rises into the air like a huge crow! The bats stream after her like a long black cape!

It's Halloween. And you can't wait to get home!

The End